MARVEL STUDIOS

THOR

THE MIGHTY AVENGER

READ-ALONG
STORYBOOK AND CD

This is the story of how Thor, the son of King Odin of Asgard, was cast away to Earth, where he became one of the realm's finest defenders. You can read along with me in your book. You will know it is time to turn the page when you hear this sound. . . . Let's begin now.

marvelkids.com

Printed in the United States of America

First Edition, October 2017
1 3 5 7 9 10 8 6 4 2
Library of Congress Control Number: 2017931620
ISBN 978-1-368-00861-7
FAC-029261-17230

PLAY TRACK 1 ON YOUR CD NOW!

It was the day of the coronation of a new king of Asgard, the mightiest of the Nine Realms of the cosmos. All of Asgard was gathered in the throne room. For centuries, the mighty Odin All-Father had defended Asgard, Earth, and the other realms from destruction and had fought to keep peace in the universe. Now King Odin's eldest son, Thor, knelt before him to accept his father's crown.

From his throne, Odin looked down proudly on his son. "And on this day, I, Odin All-Father, proclaim you . . ."

Odin's voice trailed off. He could sense that there were intruders in the weapons vault. **"Frost Giants!"**

The Frost Giants hated the Asgardians. King Odin and his army had stopped the Frost Giants from taking over Earth, driving them back to their dark icy realm of Jotunheim. There, King Odin had defeated Laufey, the king of the Frost Giants, and taken the source of their power, the Casket of Ancient Winters. Odin kept the Casket of Ancient Winters heavily guarded in Asgard so that it would never fall back into the hands of the Jotuns.

King Odin, Thor, and Loki, Odin's youngest
son, went to the vault to investigate. Three Frost Giants had
broken in and tried to steal the Casket of Ancient Winters!
Luckily, Odin's weapon, the Destroyer, had done its job and
stopped the intruders. Odin was calm, but Thor was furious.

"The Jotuns must pay for what they have done! They
broke into the weapons vault. **I want to know *why.***"

Thor wanted to attack the Frost Giants on Jotunheim, but
King Odin refused. He was still the king and he didn't want
to break the peace agreement between the Asgardians and
the Frost Giants.

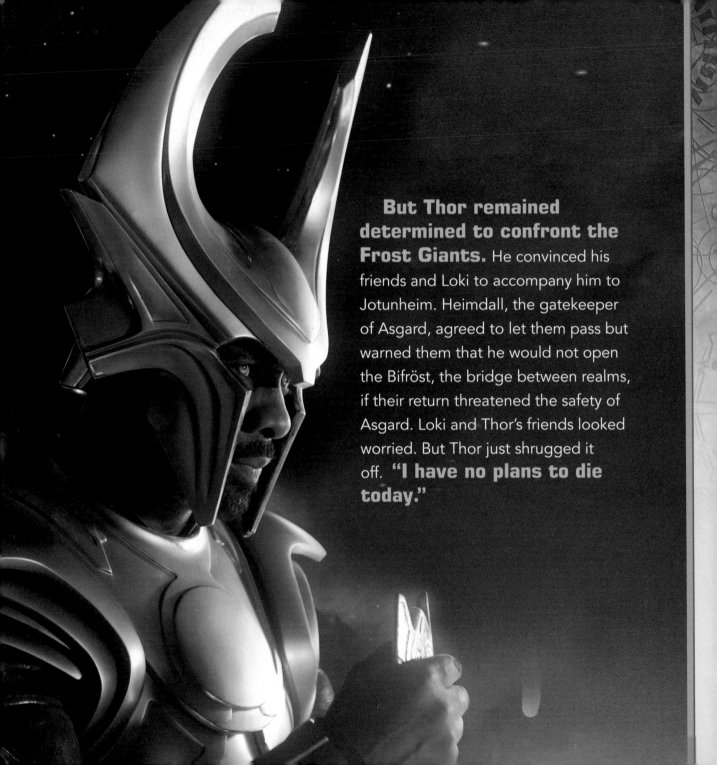

But Thor remained determined to confront the Frost Giants. He convinced his friends and Loki to accompany him to Jotunheim. Heimdall, the gatekeeper of Asgard, agreed to let them pass but warned them that he would not open the Bifröst, the bridge between realms, if their return threatened the safety of Asgard. Loki and Thor's friends looked worried. But Thor just shrugged it off. **"I have no plans to die today."**

On Jotunheim, Thor and his friends stood before Laufey, the king of the Frost Giants. When Thor asked him how the Frost Giants had forced their way into Asgard, Laufey warned of traitors in the house of King Odin. His words enraged Thor. "Do not dishonor my father's name with your lies!"

Laufey offered to let Thor and his friends leave without any consequences. Looking around at King Laufey's many guards, Loki tried to convince Thor to accept the offer and stand down. **"Thor, look around you. We're outnumbered."**

But as they turned to leave, King Laufey insulted Thor. Annoyed, Thor hurled his mighty hammer at Laufey, which drove the Frost Giants to attack the Asgardians! Together, the friends valiantly fought the Frost Giants, but King Laufey and his men trapped Thor and his friends at the edge of a cliff.

Suddenly, King Odin appeared from the sky on his horse. Thor was overjoyed.

"Father! We'll finish them together!"

But King Odin looked down on his son. "Silence!"

King Odin tried to convince King Laufey to maintain their peace agreement. "These are the actions of a boy. Treat them as such. You and I can end this here and now, before there's further bloodshed."

But King Laufey wanted to start a war.

Odin sighed. "So be it."

King Laufey raised his frosty dagger to attack King Odin. But with a burst of light, King Odin transported himself, Loki, Thor, and their friends back to Asgard.

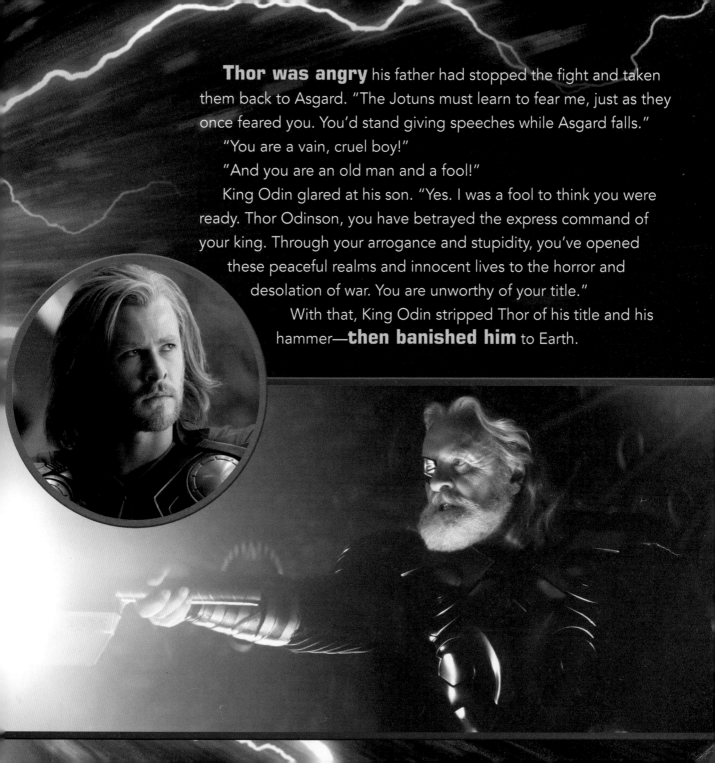

Thor was angry his father had stopped the fight and taken them back to Asgard. "The Jotuns must learn to fear me, just as they once feared you. You'd stand giving speeches while Asgard falls."

"You are a vain, cruel boy!"

"And you are an old man and a fool!"

King Odin glared at his son. "Yes. I was a fool to think you were ready. Thor Odinson, you have betrayed the express command of your king. Through your arrogance and stupidity, you've opened these peaceful realms and innocent lives to the horror and desolation of war. You are unworthy of your title."

With that, King Odin stripped Thor of his title and his hammer—**then banished him** to Earth.

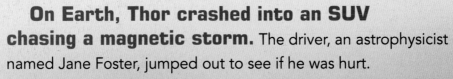

On Earth, Thor crashed into an SUV chasing a magnetic storm. The driver, an astrophysicist named Jane Foster, jumped out to see if he was hurt.

"Do me a favor and don't be dead."

Thor was dazed but uninjured. Still, Jane and her colleagues Erik Selvig and Darcy Lewis dropped Thor off at the hospital to get checked out. Thor, not understanding that the doctors were trying to help him, **pushed them away**.

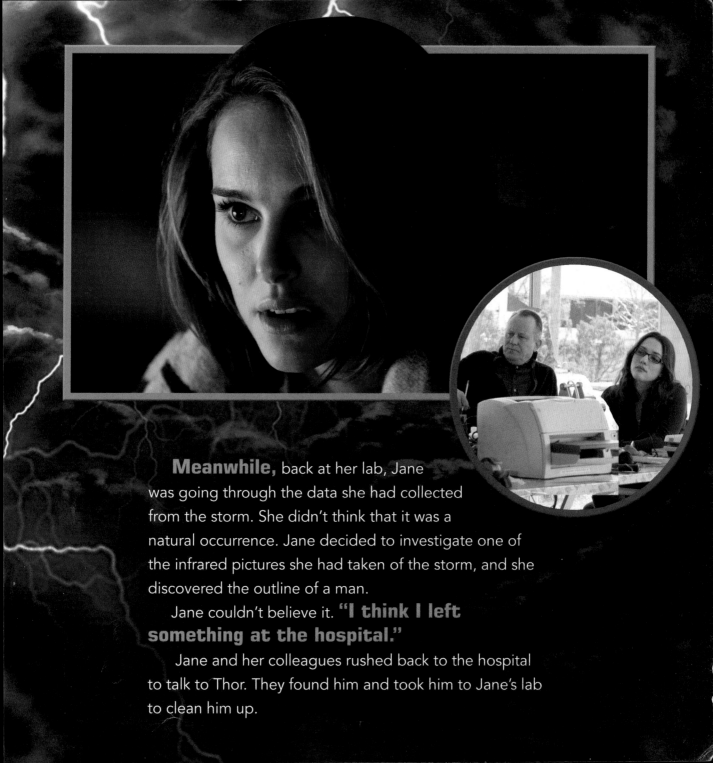

Meanwhile, back at her lab, Jane was going through the data she had collected from the storm. She didn't think that it was a natural occurrence. Jane decided to investigate one of the infrared pictures she had taken of the storm, and she discovered the outline of a man.

Jane couldn't believe it. **"I think I left something at the hospital."**

Jane and her colleagues rushed back to the hospital to talk to Thor. They found him and took him to Jane's lab to clean him up.

Back in Asgard, Loki was trying to figure something out. During the battle, one of the Frost Giants had touched his arm, turning it blue when it should have burned him. Loki went down to the vault looking for answers and picked up the Casket of Ancient Winters. When he turned around, his skin was glowing blue once again and **King Odin was standing behind him**.

Loki looked at his father. "The casket wasn't the only thing you took from Jotunheim that day, was it?"

King Odin shook his head. After the battle on Jotunheim, he had stumbled upon a newborn in the temple and taken him back to Asgard. That baby was Loki, son of King Laufey. "You were an innocent child. I thought we could unite our kingdoms one day. Bring about an alliance. Bring about permanent peace through you. But those plans no longer matter."

Loki was enraged. "It all makes sense now why you favored Thor all these years. Because no matter how much you claimed to love me, you could never have a Frost Giant sitting on the throne of Asgard."

Odin suddenly clutched his chest, collapsing on the stairs. He had fallen into the Odinsleep, and **there was no telling when he would wake**.

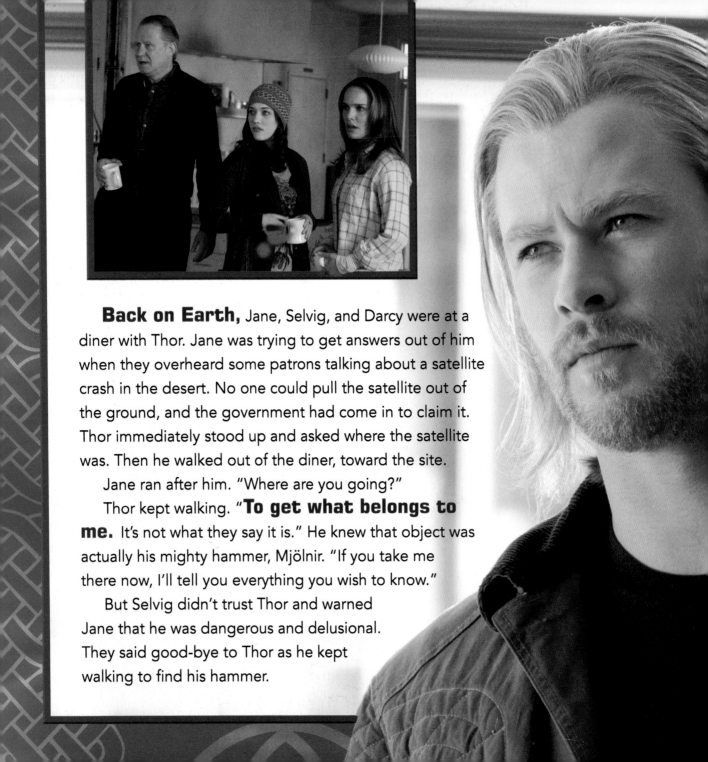

Back on Earth, Jane, Selvig, and Darcy were at a diner with Thor. Jane was trying to get answers out of him when they overheard some patrons talking about a satellite crash in the desert. No one could pull the satellite out of the ground, and the government had come in to claim it. Thor immediately stood up and asked where the satellite was. Then he walked out of the diner, toward the site.

Jane ran after him. "Where are you going?"

Thor kept walking. "**To get what belongs to me.** It's not what they say it is." He knew that object was actually his mighty hammer, Mjölnir. "If you take me there now, I'll tell you everything you wish to know."

But Selvig didn't trust Thor and warned Jane that he was dangerous and delusional. They said good-bye to Thor as he kept walking to find his hammer.

But when Jane returned to her lab, it was being ransacked. The man in charge was Agent Coulson of S.H.I.E.L.D. Coulson and his men were confiscating all of Jane's research and equipment!

Coulson offered Jane a check, which she threw to the ground. "**This is my life!** I can't just buy replacements at Radio Shack. I made most of this equipment myself. I'm on the verge of understanding something extraordinary. And everything I know about this phenomenon is either in this lab or in this book, and you can't just take this awa—Hey!"

Coulson smiled politely, then grabbed Jane's notebook out of her hand and drove away. A little later, Jane, Darcy, and Selvig sat on the roof, trying to figure out their next move.

In Asgard, Thor's friends decided to ask King Odin to reconsider Thor's banishment, but instead of their king, they found Loki sitting on the throne, wearing his ceremonial helmet.

Loki smiled down on them. "Father has fallen into the Odinsleep. Mother fears he may never awaken again. You can bring your urgent matter to me . . . your king."

Reluctantly, Thor's friends bowed before Loki
and asked him to allow Thor to come home. But Loki
refused. **"My first command cannot be
to undo the All-Father's last."**

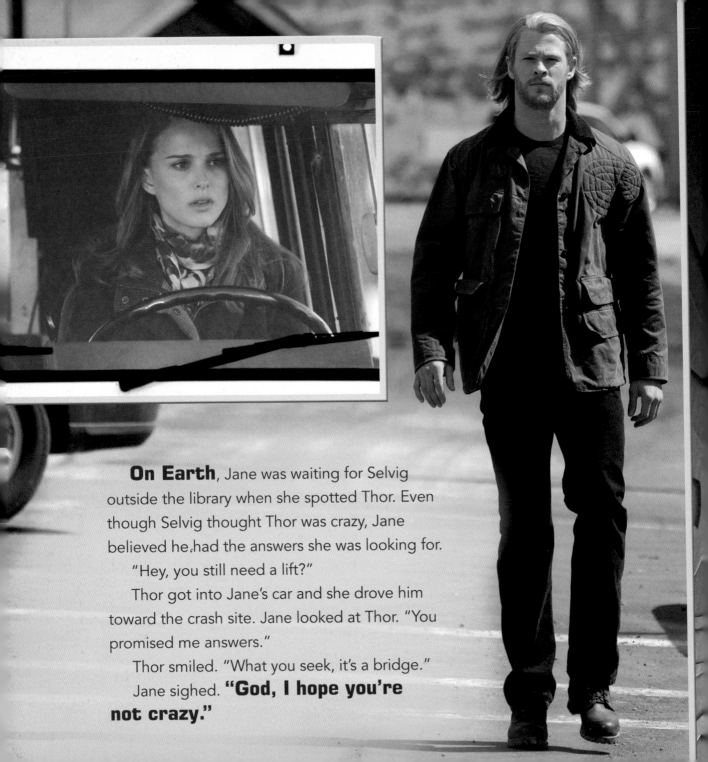

On Earth, Jane was waiting for Selvig outside the library when she spotted Thor. Even though Selvig thought Thor was crazy, Jane believed he had the answers she was looking for.

"Hey, you still need a lift?"

Thor got into Jane's car and she drove him toward the crash site. Jane looked at Thor. "You promised me answers."

Thor smiled. "What you seek, it's a bridge."

Jane sighed. **"God, I hope you're not crazy."**

When Jane and Thor reached the crash site, there was a makeshift fortress surrounded by armed guards. Jane was surprised. "That's no satellite crash. They would have hauled the wreckage away; they wouldn't have built a city around it."

Thor told Jane he was going in to get their things. Jane looked at Thor skeptically. "No, look what's down there. You think you're just gonna walk in, grab our stuff, and walk out?"

Thor grinned. **"No. I'm gonna fly out."**

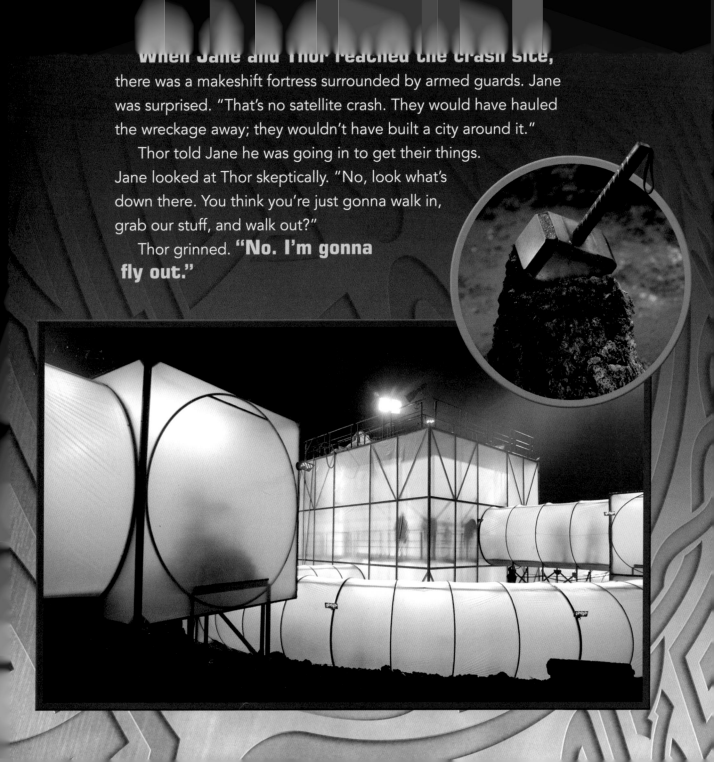

Moving quickly, Thor made his way into the fortress and knocked past the armed guards. He fought them off easily even without his superhuman strength. Then he saw his hammer stuck in the ground in the middle of the fortress. Grinning, Thor gripped the hammer's handle tightly and pulled as Agent Coulson watched. But Thor could not pick up the hammer! It remained stuck in the ground. He roared angrily at the sky and fell to his knees. Odin had placed a spell on the hammer. **Only one who was truly worthy of its power could wield it.**

With Thor distracted by his failure, Agent Coulson's men quickly moved in. They handcuffed Thor and dragged him away.

Agent Coulson started questioning Thor. Coulson believed Thor was a spy, so he wanted to know where Thor was trained and who he worked for. But Thor wouldn't answer his questions.

Coulson left the room to take a call. Suddenly, Loki appeared in front of Thor. He came bearing bad news. "Father is dead. Your banishment, the threat of a new war, it was too much for him to bear. The burden of the throne has fallen to me now."

Thor couldn't believe it. He asked Loki if he could return home. But Loki shook his head. "The truce with Jotunheim is conditional upon your exile. And Mother has forbidden your return. This is good-bye, Brother."

Thor hung his head, holding back tears. "I am sorry."

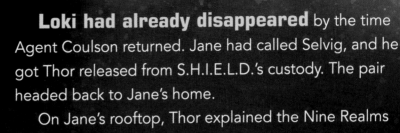

Loki had already disappeared by the time Agent Coulson returned. Jane had called Selvig, and he got Thor released from S.H.I.E.L.D.'s custody. The pair headed back to Jane's home.

On Jane's rooftop, Thor explained the Nine Realms to her, drawing a picture. "Your world is one of the Nine Realms of the cosmos, linked to each other by the branches of Yggdrasil, the World's Tree. Now you see it every day without realizing, the images glimpsed through . . . what did you call it . . . this Hubble telescope."

Jane listened, fascinated, as Thor described the other realms to her, including Asgard. **She was beginning to care for Thor.**

Meanwhile, Loki traveled to Jotunheim. He revealed to Laufey that he had let the three Frost Giants into Asgard to ruin Thor's coronation day, and he also made an offer to the king of the Frost Giants.

"I will conceal you and a handful of your soldiers, lead you into Odin's chambers, and you can slay him where he lies. Once Odin is dead, I will return the casket to you and you can return Jotunheim to all its . . . uh, glory."

Laufey accepted Loki's offer. But when Loki returned to Asgard, Heimdall was waiting at the gate with a suspicious gaze. He hadn't been able to see or hear Loki in Jotunheim.

Loki stared coldly at Heimdall. "You're sworn to obey me now. **You will open the Bifröst to no one.**"

trying to find a way to help Thor get back home when Heimdall summoned them. Since Heimdall was bound by his command to the king, he could not open the Bifröst, but **Thor's friends could**! As Heimdall turned his back and walked away, Thor's friends opened the bridge to Earth. They landed on Earth and wandered through the small town until they finally found Thor at Jane's lab.

Thor was glad to see his friends, but he told them to return to Asgard. "You should not have come. You know I cannot go home. My father is dead because of me. I must remain in exile."

His friends looked at him, confused. They told Thor his father was still alive. Loki had lied to him!

But Loki had observed Thor's friends leaving Asgard. Annoyed, he traveled down to the vault and freed the Destroyer, commanding it to get rid of Thor. "Ensure my brother does not return. **Destroy everything!**"

After that, Loki confronted Heimdall at the gates. "For your act of treason, you are relieved of your duties as gatekeeper and no longer citizen of Asgard."

Heimdall drew his sword to fight Loki, but Loki swiftly pulled out the Casket of Ancient Winters and froze Heimdall in a block of ice. Using the Bifröst, Loki sent the Destroyer down to Earth. The machine saw Coulson's S.H.I.E.L.D. agents at the hammer site. **It began blasting the agents and everything in its path!**

Thor and his friends saw the Destroyer as it approached Earth and headed toward the town. The Asgardians wanted to fight the Destroyer. But without his hammer, Thor was just a man. "I can help get these people to safety. We'll need some time."

Thor's friends agreed to distract the Destroyer while Thor and Jane evacuated the town. The Asgardians battled the Destroyer, but it was too powerful. Thor raced over to his friends. "You must return to Asgard. **You have to stop Loki.**"

His friends didn't want to leave without him, but Thor had a plan.

Leaving his friends and Jane behind, Thor walked toward the giant machine.

Thor looked up at the Destroyer. He knew that Loki could hear him on Asgard. "Brother, whatever I have done to wrong you, whatever I have done to lead you to do this, I am truly sorry. But these people are innocent. Taking their lives will gain you nothing. So take mine and end this."

The Destroyer backhanded Thor, sending him reeling. **Thor was knocked out.**

As the Destroyer turned away, Thor's hammer released itself from the ground and rocketed through the air toward Thor.

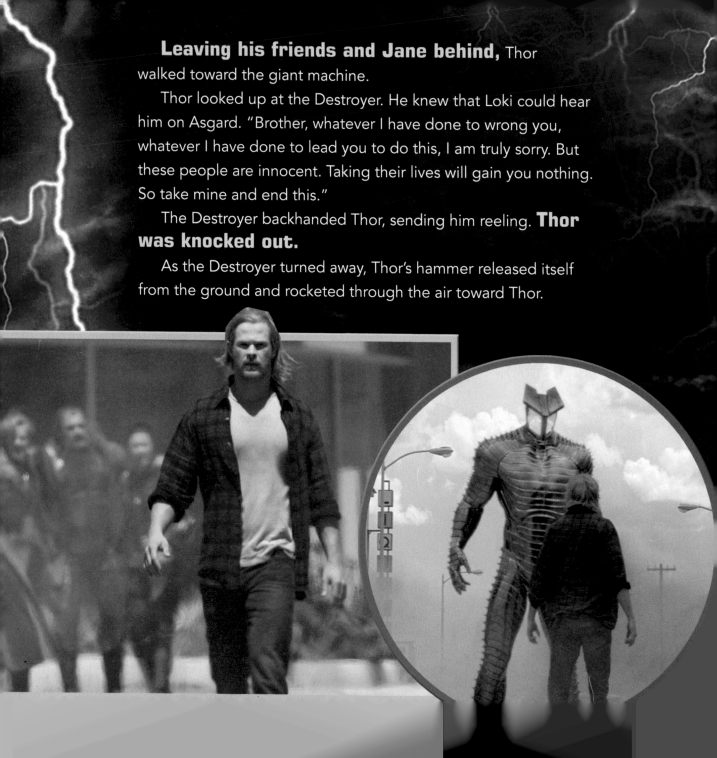

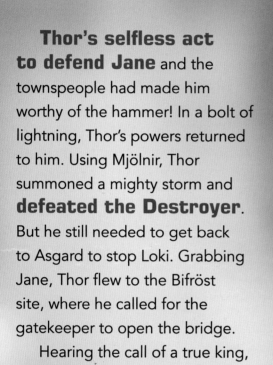

Thor's selfless act to defend Jane and the townspeople had made him worthy of the hammer! In a bolt of lightning, Thor's powers returned to him. Using Mjölnir, Thor summoned a mighty storm and **defeated the Destroyer**. But he still needed to get back to Asgard to stop Loki. Grabbing Jane, Thor flew to the Bifröst site, where he called for the gatekeeper to open the bridge.

Hearing the call of a true king, Heimdall broke through the ice and opened the gate.

Thor said good-bye to Jane. "I must go back to Asgard. But I give you my word. **I will return for you.**"

In Asgard, Loki had already let Laufey and his soldiers into the palace to kill King Odin. As Laufey knelt over the sleeping Odin, Loki blasted the Frost Giant king with his scepter, destroying him for good. "Your death came by the son of Odin."

As the queen hugged Loki, Thor appeared. "Loki. Why don't you tell her how you sent the Destroyer to kill our friends? To kill me?"

Loki grinned wickedly. "It's good to have you back. Now if you'll excuse me, I have to destroy Jotunheim." With that, a blast from Loki's scepter sent Thor hurtling through a wall.

Loki raced to the gates and opened the Bifrost to Jotunheim. Using the Casket of Ancient Winters, he blasted the Bifröst with its power, and its energy began destroying the icy realm. Desperately, Thor tried to stop it with his hammer, but it was no use. He turned to his brother. "Why have you done this?"

Loki sneered at Thor. "To prove to Father that I am the worthy son. When he wakes, I will have destroyed that race of monsters, **and I will be true heir to the throne**."

The two brothers flew toward each other. Thor trapped Loki and began to hit the Rainbow Bridge with his hammer. Before he brought down his hammer for the final blow, he paused. "Forgive me, Jane." Both brothers tumbled over the edge into space as the portal exploded and were caught by King Odin, who had awoken from the Odinsleep. But Loki let go of his father's spear and fell into space.

With Asgard and Earth both safe and Jotunheim preserved, Thor was finally able to mourn the loss of his brother, as well as his dear friend Jane. He remained hopeful that one day he would find a way to reconnect the Bifröst with Earth again and reunite with Jane. But Thor also had something to be glad about. His father, King Odin, was alive and well.

King Odin was proud of Thor. **"You'll be a wise king."**

Thor smiled. "I have much to learn. I know that now."

THOR
THE DARK WORLD

READ-ALONG
STORYBOOK AND CD

This is the story of how Thor defeated the Dark Elves and saved Jane Foster.

You can read along with me in your book. You will know it is time to turn the page when you hear this sound. . . . Let's begin now.

PLAY TRACK 2 ON YOUR CD NOW!

MARVEL

Los Angeles
New York

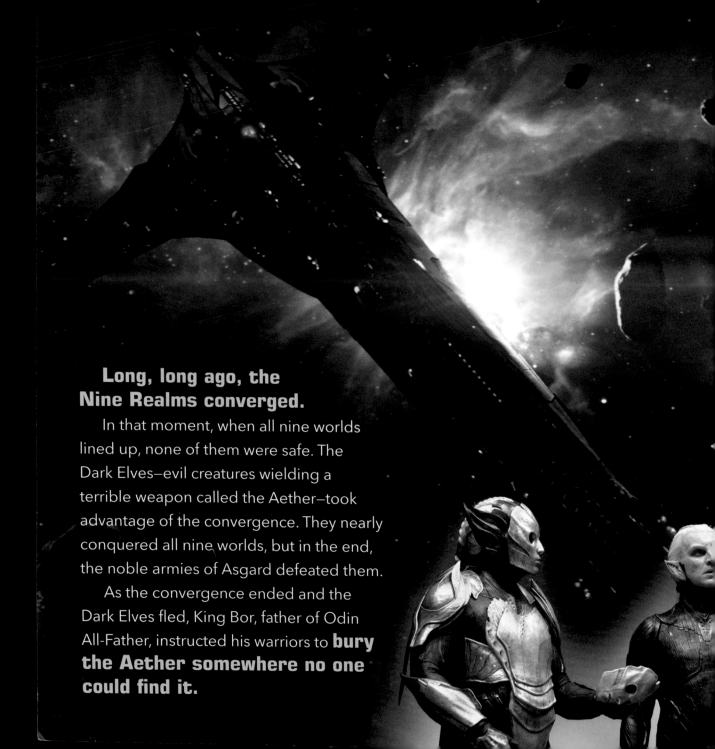

**Long, long ago, the
Nine Realms converged.**

In that moment, when all nine worlds
lined up, none of them were safe. The
Dark Elves—evil creatures wielding a
terrible weapon called the Aether—took
advantage of the convergence. They nearly
conquered all nine worlds, but in the end,
the noble armies of Asgard defeated them.

As the convergence ended and the
Dark Elves fled, King Bor, father of Odin
All-Father, instructed his warriors to **bury
the Aether somewhere no one
could find it.**

Eons later, the Dark Elves were secretly preparing for the next convergence. The Nine Realms were once more coming together. But the warriors of Asgard were distracted from this convergence by the return of Loki, the adopted brother of Thor. Loki was a trickster and a criminal, and now that he had been caught, he would have to pay for his crimes.

Odin confronted Loki in the throne room of Asgard. **"You'll spend the rest of your days in the dungeons."**

Loki sneered. "And what of Thor? You'll make that witless oaf king while I rot in chains?"

"Thor must strive to undo the damage you have done. He will bring order to the Nine Realms and then, yes, he will be king."

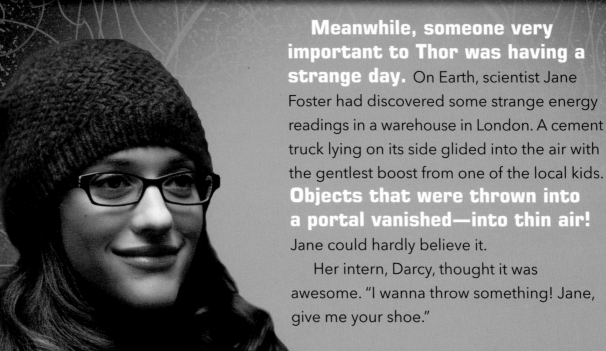

Meanwhile, someone very important to Thor was having a strange day. On Earth, scientist Jane Foster had discovered some strange energy readings in a warehouse in London. A cement truck lying on its side glided into the air with the gentlest boost from one of the local kids. **Objects that were thrown into a portal vanished—into thin air!** Jane could hardly believe it.

Her intern, Darcy, thought it was awesome. "I wanna throw something! Jane, give me your shoe."

Jane did not give Darcy her shoe. Instead, she continued her investigation. But the moment Jane wandered away from her friends, she was swept into another realm! A glowing red cloud enveloped her . . . **and soon the Aether had possessed Jane Foster!**

Jane woke up in the warehouse a few hours later, with no idea what had just happened to her. As she stepped out into the rain, she was astonished to see a tall figure in a flowing red cape.

It was Jane's true love, the Asgardian warrior Thor Odinson!

The last time Jane had seen Thor, he had promised to return for her. But he never came. Jane was angry.

"Where were you?"

Thor explained that when they last parted, the Bifröst had been destroyed. He couldn't return to Earth until now.

"Jane, I fought to protect you from the dangers of my world. But I was wrong, I was a fool. **I believe that fate brought us together.**"

The police arrived and threatened to arrest Jane for trespassing. When one tried to touch her, **a bolt of violent energy threw him away from her.** Jane collapsed again, exhausted. Alarmed, Thor whisked her off to Asgard on the Bifröst Bridge so the doctors there could examine her.

Odin was not happy to see a human in Asgard . . . not even a human that his son loved. "She does not belong here in Asgard—any more than a goat belongs at a banquet table."

Jane could hardly believe how rude he was! "Who do you think you are?"

"I am Odin. King of Asgard. Protector of the Nine Realms."

"Oh." There wasn't much Jane could say to that.

When Odin saw how Jane's body reacted to being touched by the guards, he realized she was infected with the Aether. Odin explained to Thor and Jane about the convergence and about the Aether. "It changes matter into dark matter. It seeks out host bodies, drawing strength from their life force."

Jane was the Aether's host body . . . and the Dark Elves wanted their weapon back so they could conquer the Nine Realms!

As Thor and Jane discussed the Aether in the airy balconies of the palace, down below in the dungeon, trouble was brewing.

A Dark Elf had sneaked into the palace disguised as a prisoner. Once the guards turned their backs, he let loose his powers and started a violent riot! Soon prisoners were free of their cells and fighting the guards.

Locked in his own cell, Loki ignored the chaos.

Odin wasn't concerned.
"It's a skirmish. Nothing to fear."

But just as the fight in the palace reached its peak, the sky opened up, and the cloaked ships of the Dark Elves appeared!

The ships sprayed fire in every direction, destroying many of the great towers of Asgard. The Asgardians fought back, but they were outmatched. **They'd had no warning!**

As the battle raged, the Dark Elves' leader, Malekith, stalked through the palace looking for Jane Foster. He found her being protected by Thor's mother, Frigga.

"Stand down, creature, and you may still survive this."

Frigga wasn't afraid. She fought bravely and fiercely—but Malekith struck her down.

Thor burst into the room as his mother fell. A bolt of lightning from Mjölnir struck Malekith, who turned and fled. But it was too late: **Frigga was gone.**

The Dark Elves had left, but Asgard was in ruins. The Asgardians were in shock, **but nobody was more devastated than Thor and his father.** Frigga had been a great warrior, a wise queen, and a loving wife and mother. All of Asgard mourned her loss with a magnificent funeral.

Meanwhile, the convergence was getting closer and closer. Back on Earth, Jane Foster's friend Erik Selvig was getting worried. He knew the convergence was coming, and that it would be very bad for Earth. **Luckily, he had invented a gadget that would protect the Earth from the convergence.**

"My gravimetric spikes can stabilize the focal point of the convergence. This time the alignment, and all the other worlds, would just pass us by. It's beautiful."

But nobody was listening to Erik, because he was in a mental institution.

Back on Asgard, Thor and his father couldn't agree about how to fight the Dark Elves. Odin wanted to force the Dark Elves to return to Asgard for a final battle. But Thor thought it was too dangerous—too many Asgardians would lose their lives in that battle. Odin scoffed. **"You overestimate the power of these creatures."**

"No, I value our people's lives. I'll take Jane to the Dark World and draw the enemy away from Asgard. When Malekith pulls the Aether from Jane, it will be exposed and vulnerable, and **I will destroy it and him."**

Odin forbade Thor from using his plan. But Thor knew that Odin was wrong. So he asked his most trusted friends to help him.

One of those friends was Heimdall, the keeper of the Bifröst.

Heimdall was resolute. "I cannot overrule my king's wishes. Not even for you."

But Thor kept pushing. "Malekith knew the Aether was here. He can sense its power. If we do nothing, he will come for it again but this time lay waste to all of Asgard."

Heimdall knew Thor was right. So he agreed to help with Thor's plan to use a secret passage to smuggle Jane out of Asgard.

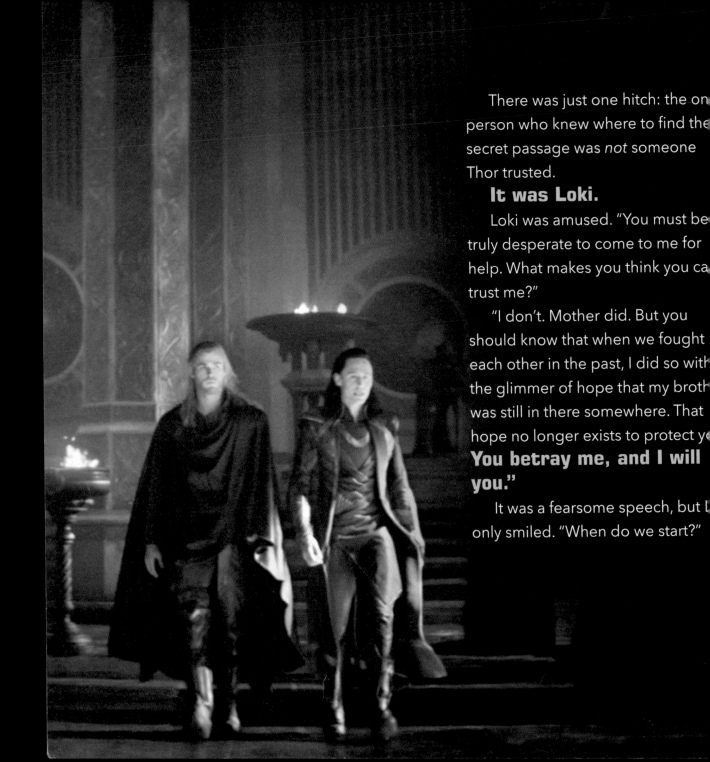

There was just one hitch: the on[e] person who knew where to find the secret passage was *not* someone Thor trusted.

It was Loki.

Loki was amused. "You must be truly desperate to come to me for help. What makes you think you ca[n] trust me?"

"I don't. Mother did. But you should know that when we fought each other in the past, I did so with the glimmer of hope that my broth[er] was still in there somewhere. That hope no longer exists to protect yo[u]. **You betray me, and I will [kill] you."**

It was a fearsome speech, but L[oki] only smiled. "When do we start?"

As Thor and Loki plotted how to get Jane to the Dark Elves, back on Earth, Darcy was plotting how to prevent the Earth from being destroyed in the convergence. The first step was getting Erik Selvig out of the mental institution. So Darcy and her intern, Ian, went to get him.

Darcy was nervous. "I should not be left in charge of stuff like this. I don't get paid enough. I don't get paid, period."

But the convergence was coming, and the laws of physics were falling apart. Darcy put a brave smile on her face. **It was time to save the world.**

At the same time, back on Asgard, **Thor and Loki began their own plan.**

Heimdall, the keeper of the Bifröst, lured Odin and his men away from the palace so that Thor and Loki could sneak out with Jane. When Odin arrived in Heimdall's chamber, he was confused.

"You called me here on an urgent matter. What is it?"

Heimdall told the truth. "Treason, my lord."

"Whose?"

"Mine."

Odin realized that he had been tricked. Thor was going to escape with Jane! He turned to his guards. **"Stop Thor. By any means necessary."**

But it was too late. Thor, Loki, and Jane stole one of the ships the Dark Elves had crashed in Asgard. It was the perfect escape plan . . . except they had no idea how to operate the ship!

Loki was unimpressed. "I thought you said you knew how to fly this thing."

Thor thumped his fist on the controls as Loki watched.

"No, don't hit it. Just press it gently."

"I *am* pressing it gently! It's not working!"

Just then the lights came on and the engine started.

Thor smiled triumphantly at his brother.

With Thor flying and Loki navigating, the brothers were able to escape Asgard and travel through a portal to Svartalfheim. **The Aether was still within Jane, consuming her life force.** She could barely keep her head up.

Svartalfheim was a bleak and broken world. The ground was covered in shattered rock and the sky looked like molten metal.

Jane looked to the horizon as the Dark Elves appeared in their ship.

The ship drew closer, bringing Malekith with it.

Thor looked at Jane and Loki. "All right, you ready?"

Loki held his still-cuffed wrists up so Thor could unlock him. Thor hesitated, and Loki rolled his eyes.

"You still don't trust me, brother?"

Thor shrugged. "Would you?" He unlocked the cuffs on Loki's wrists.

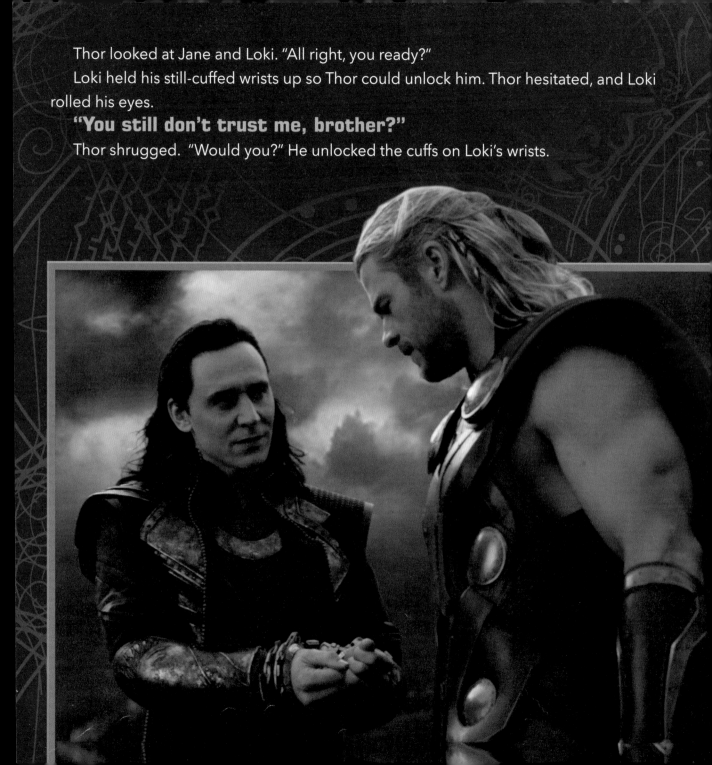

Loki didn't waste a moment. "No, I wouldn't." He moved lightning fast, attacking Thor and mortally wounding him. Then Loki grabbed Jane.

"Malekith! I am Loki of Jotunheim, and I bring you a gift!"

But Loki's double-cross was a trick! It was part of the plan. As Malekith summoned the Aether out of Jane, Thor sprang back up, unhurt.

"Loki! Now!"

Together the brothers struck the Aether as it floated in the air between Jane and Malekith. The Aether shattered into a billion pieces. But just as Thor and Loki thought they had won, the Aether came back together into a cloud and flowed into its master, Malekith.

A terrible fight ensued. Thor and Loki were outnumbered by the Dark Elves, and Thor nearly fell in battle. He was saved at the last minute by Loki, who took the blow intended for his brother. The Dark Elves left without looking back.

Loki was gone. Their plan had failed. The Dark Elves had their terrible weapon back, the convergence was about to occur, and they were stranded on the Dark World. Thor had no idea what to do.

And then, just as things seemed bleakest, Jane's cell phone started ringing. The cave was the other side of the portal Jane had discovered in London!

Before long, Thor and Jane were back in London and reunited with Darcy and Erik. **Together, the friends put the finishing touches on their plan to save the world.**

Acting fast, they found the site where the convergence would take place and began setting up Erik's equipment.

Darcy took charge. "Focus! This is important. We have to hammer them in all around the site, and then Jane and Erik will activate them from the tower."

But before they could finish setting up Erik's equipment, **Malekith arrived in a huge ship.**

The tail of the ship ground through the flagstones as it slowed to a halt. People fled, screaming, but Jane and Erik didn't run. **They knew there was no point.**

"You needn't have come so far, Asgardian. Death would've come to you soon enough."

"Not by your hand." **Thor leaped into battle.** He and Malekith traded blows of incredible power. Thor had the might of Mjölnir on his side, and Malekith had the Aether. Their fight destroyed cars and flattened trees.

As Thor kept Malekith busy, Darcy and Ian hurried to position the rest of Erik's equipment around the site of the convergence. **But they were running out of time!** Jane and Erik ran up to Thor during a lull in the fight.

"Thor! We're too late!" Jane's hair was flying wildly in the supernatural winds.

Erik nodded grimly. "Convergence is at its peak."

Overhead, a portal had opened in the sky. Through it, they could see the Nine Realms all lining up.

"We can't get close enough." Jane pointed toward where Malekith stood at the center of the convergence.

Thor straightened resolutely.
He took the posts and fought his way toward Malekith. Their final fight was brief and brutal, and as the convergence raged and a portal opened around them, Thor pinned Malekith with Erik's device. Erik flipped the switch, and Malekith disappeared.

In a blink of an eye, the Dark Elf was no more . . . and the convergence was over. **They had won.**

Back on Asgard, Thor met in private with his father.

Odin stared thoughtfully at his son. "The alignment has brought all the realms together. Every one of them saw you offer your life to save them. What can Asgard offer its new king in return?"

Thor shook his head. "Father, I cannot be king of Asgard. I will protect Asgard and all the realms with my last and every breath, but I cannot do so from that chair. Loki, for all his grave imbalance, understood rule as I know I never will. The brutality, the sacrifice . . . it changes you. **I'd rather be a good man than a great king."**

Odin nodded. "Go, my son."

"Thank you, Father."

Thor turned and left. And because his back was turned, he did not see his father's face slowly transform into the face of his trickster brother, Loki!

Loki smiled wickedly.

"No–thank *you*."

Thor didn't know it, but his life was about to get a lot more complicated!